Lindie ~~~

ies

Harvest Time

A Celebration on an Organic Farm

by Jeanne Bender
illustrated by Kate Willows

PINA PUBLISHING 🍍 SEATTLE

MAR 19

PINA PUBLISHING ᵔ SEATTLE

Text copyright © 2017 by Jeanne Bender
Illustrations by Kate Willows © 2017 by J.A. Zehrer Group, LLC
Cover and book design by Susan Harring © 2017 by J.A. Zehrer Group, LLC

For information about special discounts for bulk purchases contact:
lindielou.com/contact-us.html

Manufactured in the United States of America
Library of Congress Cataloging-in-Publication Data Bender, Jeanne

Summary:
   Lindie Lou had no idea what an organic farm was like. While visiting Cousin Ronda's farm she discovers a whole new way of living. Lindie Lou learns the importance of farming, meets up with family and friends, and the adventure begins!
   Join in the fun when Lindie Lou experiences the thrill of a hayloft, the challenge of farm animals, the puzzle of a corn maze, and the dangers of a combine.
   Lindie Lou learns life lessons while her family prepares to celebrate the harvest. Watch them play together, get in trouble together, and even save each other's lives.

ISBN: 978-1-943493-13-5 (hardcover)
ISBN: 978-1-943493-14-2 (softcover)
ISBN: 978-1-943493-15-9 (e-book)

[1. Adventure Stories. 2. Pets–Fiction. 3. Dogs–Fiction. 4. Organic Farming. 5. Agriculture–Juvenile Literature 6. Agriculture Equipment.]

Dedicated to all the amazing farm
communities around the world.
Especially,
Ronda Boyd and her Family Farm,
the Norlin and Gombert families,
the community of Anamosa, Iowa,
Bass Family Farm - Mt. Vernon, Iowa,
Geisler Family Farm - Bondurant, Iowa,
and Bhramdat family (LT Organic Farm
and Clinic) - Waukee, Iowa.

Thank you for helping us understand your
sincere effort to harvest quality crops
and manufacture nourishing produce,
necessary for life, growth and good health,
and for sustaining plentiful yields,
abundant enough to feed the world.

Lindie Lou®

You are my inspiration and the pulse of this book,
a gift to those who give it a serious look.
It may be a story of fun and appeal,
but the lessons it teaches,
are very real.

—Jeanne Bender

Here's what kids told Jeanne Bender about Lindie Lou:

Cayman and I have read the first two books. We are anxiously waiting for the third and fourth. We went back to the first book and he read the first paragraph of the book almost by himself! He now is beginning to understand what his spelling words are all about!

—Grandma Leanne, Des Moines

I had fun watching Lindie Lou and Jeanne Bender when they came to our school.

—Ian, age eleven

I'm really looking forward to this book because my family and I are farmers and because of the really cool graphics.

—RJ, age ten

My friends and I all love the Lindie Lou Series and we counted 95 la's in the Lindie Lou Song.

—Danni, age ten

I love Lindie Lou! She has fun adventures! I can't wait to read what is going to happen next.

—Eviana, age seven

DIAMOND

JASPER

RUBY

TOPAZ

LindieLou.com

Kate   Bryan

Pete

Ronda   Molly

Joe   Sherry

Curt   Angie

Mike   Vicki

Mark   Patty

Emmy Danni Lee   Ryan Krystal Bridget Rayce

VII

Contents

Chapter 1

A NEW ADVENTURE

Lindie Lou was sitting in the back seat of Bryan and Kate's car. Kate pushed a button and the car turned on. Bryan sat next to her. He was looking at a map.

Lindie Lou **LOVED** Kate and Bryan. She was happy living in Seattle and was glad they were her owners. They were very caring and made her feel safe.

The suitcases were in the back of the car. Lindie Lou didn't know where they were going, but she knew they were on another adventure.

"We should be at the airport in about forty-five minutes," said Kate. "I'd like to stop at the library. I have some books to drop off."

"Okay," replied Bryan.

Kate's little green car drove away from their house on the lake. Lindie Lou looked out the window. She saw four ducks floating on the water behind their house.

The car drove across a high bridge. Below them was the city of Seattle.

I can see the Space Needle, thought Lindie Lou. *That's where Kate took me up in space. It looks really amazing from here.*

The car took the next exit and drove through downtown Seattle.

Lindie Lou looked out the front window. Down the street was a very strange,

giant geometric building.

"We're here," announced Kate. She jumped out of the car with the pile of books under her arm. Kate ran up to a book drop-off area on the outside of the building.

"Hello," said a recording. It was coming from a loudspeaker in the wall. "Please open the door and place your books on the belt."

Kate did as she was told. Lindie Lou watched the books move up the belt and drop into a large box hanging from the ceiling.

Wow, thought Lindie Lou. *What a cool system.* She looked up at the building.

This amazing looking building must be the Seattle Public Library.

Kate jumped back into the car.

"Okay, errand complete," she said.

"On to the

,"

announced Bryan.

Chapter 2

GUESS WHO ELSE IS COMING?

"We're going to the airport!" barked Lindie Lou. She liked airports. Her friend Max taught her not to be afraid of airports or airplanes. He taught her a lot of other wise things too.

I wonder where we're going this time, thought Lindie Lou.

"Are Joe and Sherry coming?" asked Bryan.

"Yes," replied Kate. "My sister Sherry wouldn't miss Cousin Ronda's harvest party. She goes every year."

JOE AND SHERRY* are *coming? thought Lindie Lou. *I get to see Joe and Sherry again?*

Joe and Sherry raised Lindie Lou in the city of Saint Louis. She lived there with her mom Molly and her brothers and sisters. They grew up in a Puppy Playground. When Lindie Lou was old

enough to travel, Joe and Sherry flew
her to Seattle, where she now lived
with Kate and Bryan.

Lindie Lou was so excited she jumped
up and down in her travel carrier.

"You remember Joe and Sherry,
don't you, girl?" asked Bryan. He turned
and looked at Lindie Lou. "Guess who
else is coming?"

"**JASPER,**" said Bryan.

Jasper was Lindie Lou's brother. He still lived with Joe, Sherry, and their mom, Molly.

"Woo-hoo," howled Lindie Lou.

Kate and Bryan laughed.

The last time Lindie Lou saw Jasper, they were together in the Puppy Playground, playing the

sliding game.

Her brother Topaz and sisters Ruby and Diamond also liked to play the

sliding game. Lindie Lou wondered if they played the sliding game at their new homes too.

The car pulled off the main road, drove a few more miles, and then entered Sea-Tac Airport.

"We're almost there," said Kate.

Lindie Lou saw airplanes taking off into the sky.

The car pulled up to a moving walkway. Bryan and Kate jumped out.

"I'll get the luggage," said Bryan.

"Okay," replied Kate. "I'll bring Lindie Lou."

Bryan loaded their luggage onto the walkway, while Kate's self-parking car found an empty parking space. Kate lifted Lindie Lou's carrier onto the walkway. Bryan stepped on too. They were moving through a security

scanner and over to the luggage drop-off area. After passing security Bryan stepped off the walkway and rolled their suitcases over to a conveyer belt. Kate lifted Lindie Lou's carrier off of the walkway and looked up at a sign.

"Let's go to the gate," she said. Kate pulled Lindie Lou, in her carrier, past many colorful shops and restaurants.

"Our flight is on time," said Bryan.

He found them a seat near the gate.

"Ronda just left us a message," said Kate. "She'll be waiting for us at the baggage claim area in the Des Moines airport."

"Great," replied Bryan.

"Flight number 1226, to Des Moines, Iowa is ready for boarding," said a voice over the loudspeaker.

Kate followed Bryan down a ramp and onto the airplane. When they reached their seats, Bryan pushed a button on Lindie Lou's carrier. The handle slid down and the carrier wrapped around Lindie Lou like a blanket.

"Lindie Lou's carrier will fit under the seat in front of me," said Kate. "There's plenty of room."

"Okay," said Bryan. He rolled Lindie Lou under the seat.

Lindie Lou was lying down, with her

head sticking out. She rested her chin on one of her **huge** front paws.

I like flying with Kate and Bryan, thought Lindie Lou.

The rumble of the airplane's engines made her feel sleepy. While passengers found their seats, Lindie Lou fell

sound asleep.

z z Z

Chapter 3

WHERE EVERYTHING GROWS

THUD was the sound the airplane made when it landed. Lindie Lou woke up from a deep sleep.

SWOOSH was the sound the plane made as it slowed down. Then the plane rolled along the runway.

We've landed, thought Lindie Lou. She looked up at Kate, who was looking out the window.

"It's a beautiful October day in Des Moines, Iowa," said Kate.

"It sure is," replied Bryan. He reached down, lifted Lindie Lou out of her carrier, and sat her up on Kate's lap.

"Did you enjoy the ride?" asked Bryan. Lindie Lou looked up at him, tipped her head, and smiled.

"I can see a pumpkin patch in the distance," said Kate.

Bryan leaned toward Kate and looked out the window.

"Hey, look over there!"

Bryan pointed to a large machine moving through a soybean field.

"It's a combine," said Bryan.

Lindie Lou looked out the window.

That combine sure is big, thought Lindie Lou.

The plane came to a stop. Bryan waited for the aisle to clear. He stood up, lifted Lindie Lou from Kate's lap, and placed her back in her travel carrier. Bryan pulled Lindie Lou down the aisle and off the plane. A sign saying baggage claim led them toward the exit.

"Ya-hoo-ee" came a loud voice from a crowd in the baggage claim area.

Lindie Lou saw a woman jumping up and down.

"Welcome to Iowa, where everything grows!"

"It's Cousin Ronda," yelled Kate. She ran and hugged her so tightly that Ronda squealed.

Cousin Ronda had shoulder-length blonde hair, rosy cheeks, and bright-blue

eyes. She was wearing a purple plaid
shirt, blue jeans, and cowboy boots.

Bryan walked over with Lindie Lou
and their suitcases. He stretched out

his long arms and pulled Ronda and Kate into a bear hug.

"It's great to see you again," said Bryan.

Ronda hugged them both, then turned and looked at Lindie Lou.

"So this is Li'l Lindie Lou," said Ronda.

Lindie Lou looked up at Ronda and tipped her head.

"She sure is a cutie."

Ronda squatted down.

"Look at those **big green** eyes."

Lindie Lou put her paws on the front of her pet carrier and leaned toward Ronda.

"Oh, my," giggled Ronda. "Look at your **huge** paws. Where in the world did you get these?" Ronda reached for one of Lindie Lou's paws. Lindie Lou leaned over and licked Ronda's nose.

"Lindie Lou's father has huge paws, just like hers," said Kate.

"Well, isn't she special," said Ronda. She stood up and put her hands on her hips. "Lindie Lou, did you know your brother Topaz lives with me? His fur has turned a pretty golden color and he's quite the trouble-maker."

"Topaz!" barked Lindie Lou. Lindie Lou remembered playing with her brother in the Puppy Playground. She remembered Topaz jumping into a box of stuffed animals. He grabbed a gray mouse, tore a hole in it, then pulled its stuffing out.

"Topaz likes to chase mice on the farm," said Ronda.

He hasn't changed, thought Lindie Lou.

"Well, come on now. Let's get you over to the farm. My husband Pete is waiting for us. He's looking forward to meeting you."

Ronda grabbed the handle of Lindie Lou's carrier and rushed toward the exit. Kate and Bryan followed with their suitcases.

Chapter 4

NEVER A DULL MOO-MENT

"How do you like my wheels?" asked Ronda. She ran over to a bright-purple, ten-passenger van. "I call it the Party Barge. It's big like a barge and when I fill it with people, they're always in the mood to party."

"Nice," replied Bryan.

Ronda pushed a button and the doors slid open.

"Hop in," said Ronda.

Bryan stacked the luggage on the floor in the back of the van, lifted Lindie Lou onto one of the seats, and jumped in next to her. Kate climbed in the front seat, next to Ronda.

"Here we go!" yelled Ronda.

The Party Barge drove away from the airport and onto a country road. Lindie Lou looked out the window.

It was a sunny, autumn afternoon. The farmland was covered with yellow cornstalks and brown soybean plants. Green pastures grew around bright-red barns. The fields rolled up hillsides and down small country roads. The land *stretched* as far as Lindie Lou could see.

"You see more land than houses in this part of the state," said Ronda. Kate and Bryan nodded.

"There's my friend Patty's farm," said Ronda. "Patty and her husband Mark raise **Angus** cattle. Have you ever seen a COW, Lindie Lou?"

Lindie Lou looked at the field next to Mark and Patty's barn. She saw several black cows standing on the hillside. They were eating grass and looked very *peaceful.*

"Those cows are free to roam," said Ronda. "They eat only the best... and are the best of the best."

Ronda pulled the van over to the side of the road.

"There's Mark's prize-winning bull," said Ronda. She pointed to the biggest one in the herd.

Ronda opened her window and leaned out. She held her hands up to her mouth and said, "**moooooo.**" She **mooooed** again. She mooed so loud, the bull turned his head and looked at her.

"He thinks this van is a bull," laughed Ronda.

Kate and Bryan looked at each other. Lindie Lou looked at the bull.

"He doesn't look very friendly," said Bryan.

"Actually, he looks angry," said Kate.

The bull lifted his front hoof, dug it into the ground, and threw the dirt back behind him. Then, he did it again.

"He looks like he's going to charge," gasped Kate.

"Oh, he'll charge us alright," said Ronda. She let out an even louder

maa-oooo.

The bull started to run down the hill toward the van.

"Watch this," said Ronda. She drove the van very slowly, then a little faster. She stuck her head out her open window and **mooed** again.

The bull picked up speed.

"He's protecting the cows," said Ronda.

Kate, Bryan, and Lindie Lou watched the bull run after the van. Steam was coming out of his nostrils. His eyes were dark and angry and his tail was swaying wildly in the air.

Lindie Lou jumped into Bryan's lap and peered over his shoulder. She was

SHAKING.

Ronda put her head up and let out another big loud...

"maa-oooo-ee."

The bull ran even faster.

He was about to ram the back of Ronda's van when she stepped on the gas and sped away.

"He almost rammed us," said Kate.

"Wouldn't be the first time," howled Ronda.

"Never a dull moment with Ronda," said Bryan.

"You mean

m**-ment,"**

laughed Kate.

Lindie Lou watched the bull. It stopped in the middle of the road.

When the van was a safe distance away, the bull turned and walked back to his herd.

The Party Barge

SPED OFF

into the distance.

Chapter 5

AS FAR AS YOU CAN SEE

"Look to the right. It's Curt and Angie's farm," said Ronda. "Curt and my husband Pete are cousins. Their family moved here six months ago from Ohio. They have twelve kids. Four of them are adopted. They also have two dozen silkies," said Ronda.

"What's a silkie?" asked Kate.

"A silkie is a **fuzzy** chicken. They are the **CUTEST, SOFTEST, SWEETEST** chickens you'll ever see.

They have **FLUFFY** heads and **big,** feathery feet."

Bryan held up one of Lindie Lou's feet. "Like this?"

Ronda looked through the rear-view mirror.

"Yup." She laughed. "If Lindie Lou walked into the chicken coop, it would be hard to tell her from the silkies."

They all laughed.

"Look, there's Angie."

Ronda rolled down her window and stuck her arm out. She waved in a

BIG CIRCLE.

"Hi, Angie," yelled Ronda.

Angie waved back.

Angie stood between a two-story white house and a vegetable garden. Four of her children were playing on the lawn with a  chicken. Behind the house was a large red barn. Next to the barn was a giant cornfield.

Kate and Bryan waved too.

"Do you see their garden?" asked Ronda.

"Yes," said Bryan.

"Curt grows really tasty organic food in there."

"Will we get a chance to see it up close?" asked Bryan.

"You sure will," replied Ronda. "We're going over in a day or two to help pick vegetables for the harvest party."

"Great," said Kate.

"What kind of vegetables are they growing?" asked Bryan.

"It's a seasonal farm," replied Ronda. "Right now they're harvesting squash, eggplant, potatoes, and carrots. I picked some ripe heirloom tomatoes the other day too."

"Sounds yummy," said Kate.

"I'll explain more about organic farming during your visit."

"Great," said Bryan.

The Party Barge drove up another

hill. The road wound around many acres of farmland.

"Who owns all this land?" asked Kate.

"Lots of people," replied Ronda. "I own the land on this side of the road." She pointed to the left. "My neighbors, Vicki and Mike own the land on the other side. I'm growing soybeans this year and they're growing corn."

"Are those soybean plants?" asked Kate. "They're brown. I thought they'd be green."

"They're green in the summer and brown in the autumn," replied Ronda.

Ronda drove the Party Barge onto a

dirt road and stopped near her soybean field. She opened the doors and jumped out.

"Let me show you a soybean," she said. Kate, Bryan, and Lindie Lou jumped out of the van. They followed Ronda into the field.

"Here's a soybean," said Ronda. She picked one of the pods from one of the plants, squeezed the dry outer skin with her fingers, and the soybeans ROLLED into her hand. "These pods are actually a fruit," said Ronda.

"They look like beans to me," said Bryan.

"They sure do," agreed Kate.

"You're both right," replied Ronda. "The outer pod is the fruit part. The beans grow inside the pod."

"So it's a fruit AND a bean?" said Kate.

"Yes," replied Ronda. She handed each of them a few beans. "The word *bean* is a common name for a large seed. Another common name is *legume*."

"Can we eat them?" asked Kate.

"If you eat them raw, they could make you **sick**," replied Ronda. "But if you cook them, they are a good source of protein and fiber."

"You've just learned a new lesson, Lindie Lou," said Bryan.

"Don't eat anything growing in the wild until you check with an adult."

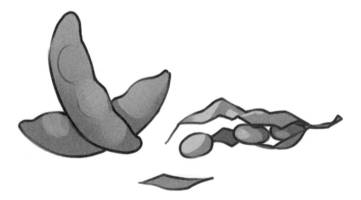

Lindie Lou walked over to Bryan. He held out his hand and let her smell the soybeans. Lindie Lou wrinkled her nose and walked away.

Ronda *tossed* her beans back into the field. So did Kate and Bryan.

"How much of this land belongs to you?" asked Bryan.

Ronda waved her arms in the air.

"As far as you can **see**."

"Farther than those hills?" asked Kate.

"Yup," said Ronda. "I was given this land by my father, who got it from his father. We've been farming this land for three generations."

Ronda turned and walked back toward the van.

"There are smaller farms around here too," said Ronda. "Most of them are organic, similar to Curt and Angie's garden. Organic food is sold to local stores and nearby farmers' markets."

"Interesting," said Kate. They followed Ronda back toward the van.

"It looks like you, Vicki, and Mike grew a lot of food this year," said Bryan.

"Yes," replied Ronda. "We had a very good year. Next year Vicki and Mike will grow soybeans and I'll grow corn. We **rotate** the crops. It keeps the soil healthy."

"Smart," said Kate.

"Hey, wait a minute," said Bryan. He looked at their feet. "Where's Lindie Lou?"

They all stopped and looked around the soybean field.

Lindie Lou was

gone!

Chapter 6

WHAT ARE YOU DOING HERE?

Lindie Lou liked being in a soybean field. It smelled of crisp leaves and dry soil. The leaves reminded her of when she lived in Saint Louis. The first time she stepped on **crunchy** leaves, she liked the sound they made. Lindie Lou kicked some of the leaves up into the air. They landed on her head.

I wonder how I look with leaves on my head, she thought. *Maybe I look like a soybean plant.*

Lindie Lou kept walking between the plants. They were higher than her head, so she couldn't see much. But she didn't care, she liked walking through the plants anyway.

Lindie Lou wove her way through the field. She was happy because she was free. She lifted her head and bit a bean pod off one of the plants. Then Lindie Lou stopped.

I'm not supposed to eat soybeans, thought Lindie Lou. She spit the pod out. *Good thing I learned this lesson today.*

Lindie Lou kept walking. She found a large pile of leaves. She dug a hole in the middle, then crawled inside. Lindie Lou liked being all covered up with leaves. She pushed her way through the pile, nudging the leaves aside with her nose.

After a while, Lindie Lou stopped to see where she was. She sat up. Her head **popped** out of the top of the leaf pile. Lindie Lou looked around.

The soybean field was so big; it was all she could see. Lindie Lou realized she didn't know where she was. Everywhere

she looked, all she could see were soybean plants and more soybeans.

Hmm, thought Lindie Lou. *I better find out where I am.* She **jumped up** and tried to look above the plants, but Lindie Lou was too short. She tried to climb up one of the stalks, but it was too **brittle**. It broke in half and she fell back down to the ground. She simply couldn't see where she was.

Lindie Lou sat down.

What should I do? she wondered.

Lindie Lou looked up at the sky. Black crows were circling above her. One of the crows swooped down into the field. It picked up a mouse and flew away with the mouse in its mouth.

Gosh, thought Lindie Lou. *This reminds me of the time my brother Topaz jumped into the box of stuffed animals and tore a little mouse into pieces.*

All of a sudden Lindie Lou didn't want to be in the soybean field anymore. She looked up at the sky again.

More crows were *circling* above.

I think I'm too big for them to pick up, thought Lindie Lou. *I sure hope so.*

Just then a gray mouse ran past her feet. Then another one. Then three more. Lindie Lou heard something running through the field. A yellow dog rushed past her. It was chasing the mice.

Could it be..., thought Lindie Lou.

"TOPAZ???"

barked Lindie Lou.

The dog stopped running. Lindie Lou heard the leaves rustling as the dog turned around. She could hear it walking back toward her. The dog stuck its head through the soybean plants and looked at Lindie Lou.

"Is that you, Lindie Lou?"

Lindie Lou was so excited to see Topaz she ran circles around him. Topaz's head spun around like a yo-yo. He was watching Lindie Lou.

"It's not like... I'm not happy to see you, but... what are you doing here?" asked Topaz.

"I'm here with my new owners, Kate and Bryan," said Lindie Lou. "They're visiting Cousin Ronda. We're here for the harvest party."

"Awesome," barked Topaz. "Pete and Ronda are MY new owners."

"I like Ronda. I haven't met Pete yet," said Lindie Lou. "What's it like living on a farm?"

"Come on, I'll show you," replied

Topaz. "There are lots of places to run and play." He turned and walked down a path. "I'm pretty much free to go anywhere I like."

"Wait a minute," said Lindie Lou. Topaz stopped and turned around. "Are you going to catch any more mice? I don't like to see them get hurt."

"I mostly chase them. I don't catch very many," said Topaz.

"Isn't catching mice a cat's job?" asked Lindie Lou.

"Yes, it is," replied Topaz. "But there are plenty of mice for all of us. If we don't catch them, they'll eat up all the soybeans."

Lindie Lou had a **sad** look on her face.

"Okay, I promise," said Topaz. "As long as you're here, I won't catch any mice."

Lindie Lou smiled.

"Is it okay if I chase them?" asked Topaz. "I like the race."

"Okay," said Lindie Lou.

"Come on then. Let me show you around."

Lindie Lou followed Topaz through the field. He led her over to a bright-pink barn with white trim.

"This is Pete and Ronda's farm," said Topaz.

"The barn is pink," said Lindie Lou.

"Yes, it is," replied Topaz. "It's Ronda's favorite color. "Her other favorite color is **purple**."

"It sure is bright," said Lindie Lou.

"She likes it that way," replied Topaz.

"Come on, Lindie Lou. Let me show you where I live."

Topaz led Lindie Lou through a crack in the side of the barn.

Chapter 7

THE HAYLOFT

Lindie Lou followed Topaz into the barn. She had never been in a barn before. She saw a large green tractor parked near the door. Bales of HAY were stacked near the tractor.

"This way," said Topaz.

Lindie Lou followed Topaz to the back of the barn and up a **narrow wooden** staircase to a pile of hay.

"This is where I sleep," said Topaz.

"In this?" asked Lindie Lou.

"It's called HAY," said Topaz. "Pete and Ronda grow it in one of their fields."

Lindie Lou sniffed the hay.

"First, they plant rye grass," said Topaz. "Then it is cut, dried, and bundled. The dry grass is called hay. Pete and Ronda sell it to Mark and Patty, who feed it to their cattle."

Lindie Lou looked around.

"Where's your bed?"

"Over here," said Topaz. He climbed on top of the pile of hay, dug a hole in the middle, and sat down. "This is my bed."

Lindie Lou climbed up on the pile of hay. She dug a hole next to Topaz and sat down.

"Can I sleep here with you?"

"Sure," said Topaz. He looked around the room. "Do you want to have some fun?"

"Yes!" said Lindie Lou.

Topaz jumped down from the pile of hay and ran to an opening in the floor.

"**Be careful,**" warned Lindie Lou. "**You might fall.**"

"See yah," yelled Topaz. He jumped up into the air, then fell down through a hole in the floor.

"Topaz?" barked Lindie Lou. "Are you all right?" She ran over and looked down through the hole.

Topaz was lying on a large, soft pile of hay. He was

"It's your turn, Lindie Lou."

"What if I jump and miss the hay?" asked Lindie Lou.

"Don't be a scaredy-cat," said Topaz. "You won't miss the pile. It's too big."

Lindie Lou looked very carefully at the pile of hay. Topaz was right. It *was* a big pile, and it looked *very* soft.

"Okay, here goes."

Lindie Lou closed her eyes and jumped. She landed right in the middle of the pile. Lindie Lou rolled over and was all covered in HAY.

"You look like a scarecrow," laughed Topaz.

"What's a scarecrow?" asked Lindie Lou. She **shook** the hay off her fur.

"Come take a look," said Topaz.

He led Lindie Lou back up the stairs and over to a window. A stick figure,

dressed in a red shirt and overalls, hung on a pole in the middle of a cornfield.

"That's a scarecrow," said Topaz. "Farmers put them in their fields to scare the crows away."

Lindie Lou looked out the window.

"Very smart," she said.

Topaz **ran** to the edge of the hayloft.

"Don't do this at home," he yelled.

Lindie Lou turned around just in time to see him jump off the edge. She ran to the opening.

This time Topaz stretched his arms out. His back legs were straight and his toes were pointed. Just before he hit the hay, Topaz twisted in the air, and landed on his back.

"How was that?"

"Awesome," barked Lindie Lou. "Now it's my turn."

Lindie Lou jumped through the hole. She stuck out all four of her legs. Just before she landed, she flipped over twice and ended up on her tummy. Her legs were all spread out. She looked like a brown **FURRY** rug.

"That was good," barked Topaz.

Lindie Lou and Topaz ran up the stairs again. They jumped many more times. Each time they made different patterns in the air.

"Let's jump together!" barked Lindie Lou.

"Okay," replied Topaz.

They ran to one end of the barn, turned around, and ran to the opening in the hayloft. Together they jumped off the edge, did a few flips in the air, and just before they landed, Kate, Bryan, Ronda, and Pete walked in.

"There's Lindie Lou," said Bryan.

"Those puppies look like they're diving in the Olympics," giggled Ronda.

"Lindie Lou, we were worried about you," said Kate. "It's a good thing I was able to track you with this." Kate held up a small, square, remote tracking device.

Lindie Lou ran over to Kate, jumped into her arms and licked her cheek.

"You look like a little, prickly  **PORCUPINE**," said Bryan.

Kate picked the hay out of her fur.

"I see you found Topaz," said Ronda. She knelt down and whistled.

Topaz ran and jumped into Ronda's arms.

"Make that two **PORCUPINES**," said Ronda.

"Kate and Bryan, meet Topaz," said Ronda's husband, Pete.

"So, you're Lindie Lou's brother," said Bryan. He rubbed Topaz's head.

Ronda picked the hay out of Topaz's fur. "Now that we've found Lindie Lou, let us show you to your room," said Ronda.

Ronda and Pete led Kate and Bryan to a door on the other side of the barn. Inside was a **cozy** bedroom and bath.

"We call this the harvest room," said Ronda.

On the curtains and the bedspread, were images of the four crops, farmers grow to feed the world.

Corn, Wheat, Soy, and Rice.

"What a great tribute to the farm effort," said Bryan.

"Thanks," replied Pete.

"You'd better get unpacked," said Ronda. "After supper we plan to go right to bed. We rise very early on the farm. The roosters wake us up."

"Okay," replied Kate.

"Mark and Patty are expecting us at their farm early tomorrow morning," said Ronda. "When we get there, I have a surprise for you."

Chapter 8

LOOK WHO'S HERE

The next morning the rooster woke them up. They climbed into Ronda's bright-purple Party Barge and drove down several roads and around many turns.

Lindie Lou put her paws on the edge of the window. She jumped up to see the beautiful fall colors.

"We're almost there," said Ronda. The van made another wide turn.

"There's Mark and Patty," said Ronda.

She opened her window and waved her hand in a big circle.

Mark and Patty were standing in front of their barn. They waved back.

The Party Barge pulled into the driveway. It passed the barn and stopped at their yellow farmhouse. Mark and Patty's black Angus **COWS** were grazing in the field.

"Should we go over and say 'hi' to your friend, the bull?" asked Bryan.

Ronda looked at the bull.

"Maybe later," replied Ronda. "He's too busy eating the hay I brought him. And besides, I don't want to wear him out."

Everyone laughed and jumped out of the van. Mark and Patty walked over to greet them.

"Meet my cousins, Kate and Bryan," said Ronda.

"Hi, Kate. Hi, Bryan," said Patty.

"Welcome to our farm," said Mark. He shook Bryan's and Kate's hands.

"This is Li'l Lindie Lou," said Ronda.

Patty looked down at Lindie Lou.

"She sure is a **FUZZY** little thing," said Patty. She bent down and petted Lindie Lou. "Come on into the house. Someone wants to say 'hi.'" Patty led everyone through the front door of their farmhouse.

"**Surprise!**" said Ronda. "Look who's here."

"Hey, hi!" said Kate. She walked over and gave them a hug. Bryan shook their hands.

"I see you brought Lindie Lou's brother, Jasper, and her mom, Molly with you," said Bryan. He bent down and petted both of them.

"So this is Jasper," said Kate. "I hear you're the PLAYFUL puppy."

Lindie Lou peeked around Bryan. Her eyes grew bigger when she saw

SHERRY, JOE, MOLLY, and JASPER.

Lindie Lou was so happy she almost knocked a lamp over while running to greet them.

"I wondered if I'd ever see you again," barked Lindie Lou.

Molly and Lindie Lou ran in circles around each other. Jasper jumped off of Sherry's lap and joined them. They were so happy to be together again. Lindie Lou rolled on her back. Molly and Jasper nuzzled up against her. Lindie Lou's **big** paws bobbed in the air.

"Hey, Lindie Lou," said Joe. "Remember me?" He reached down and rubbed Lindie Lou's tummy.

"You've grown a bit," said Sherry. She bent down and touched the medal hanging from Lindie Lou's collar. "I see you still have the collar I gave you." Sherry smiled. Lindie Lou looked up at her and licked her hand.

"Hey, guess who else is here?" said Lindie Lou to Jasper.

"Who?" asked Jasper.

"Our brother, Topaz."

"Where is he?" asked Jasper. He looked around the room.

"He lives down the road in Pete and Ronda's barn."

"When can we see him?" asked Molly.

"How about now?" said a voice in the back of the room.

Topaz walked around the side of the sofa.

"I heard Ronda say something about a surprise. So I decided to run over here and see what all the fuss was about."

"It's Joe, Sherry, Molly, and Jasper," said Lindie Lou.

"Oh wow! Hey! Hi!" said Topaz.

"Hi, Topaz," said Jasper. They touched noses, then sniffed each other.

Molly ran over to Topaz. "It's great to see you, Son. I see your fur has turned a nice yellow color." Molly sniffed him too.

Topaz was so happy to see them he did a back-flip in the air. Then he ran in circles around Jasper. Topaz ran so fast he almost knocked Ronda over.

"I think there are too many dogs in here," announced Ronda. "It's time for you to go **outside** and play."

"But first, I have treats," said Patty. She held up a handful of homemade soy biscuits. "Sit."

All four dogs sat at Patty's feet.

"Good," said Patty. She went over, opened the door, and tossed the treats onto the lawn.

Molly and her puppies ran outside.

"What a nice place to live," said Molly.

"It sure is," replied Topaz.

"There is so much SPACE," said Jasper. "I bet there are a lot of things to do here."

"There sure are," replied Topaz. "Hey, come with me. I have something to show you."

Topaz led Jasper, Lindie Lou, and Molly behind Mark and Patty's house, toward a cornfield.

Chapter 9

THE CORN MAZE

Topaz stopped near the side of Mark and Patty's cornfield.

"This is the way in," he said.

"The way in where?" asked Lindie Lou.

"Into the corn maze," replied Topaz.

"What's a corn **MAZE?**" asked Lindie Lou.

"It's a trail in a cornfield. There is an entrance, a center, and an exit. It's kind of like... a **PUZZLE.** Once you're inside, you have to find your way out."

"Let's go," barked Jasper. He ran past Topaz, picked a path, and disappeared into the maze.

Molly walked over to the entrance of the corn maze. "This isn't for me," she said. "I think I'll stay here."

"Come on, Lindie Lou," barked Topaz. He turned and ran after Jasper.

Lindie Lou watched Topaz disappear down the path. Then, she turned to Molly.

"Instead of staying here, I'm going to find the exit and wait for you there," said Molly.

"Okay," replied Lindie Lou.

Lindie Lou smiled at Molly, turned

around, and ran into the maze. She ran down a winding path and around a corner. At the end of the path, it split in two directions.

Now what? thought Lindie Lou. She looked both ways.

I know. I'm just going to stop worrying and have some fun.

Lindie Lou chose one of the paths. She ran as fast as she could. Every time she had to make a decision, she just turned and kept running.

I never thought getting lost could be so much fun.

Lindie Lou ran down another path and around another corner. She was running so  she didn't see Topaz and ran right into him.

"Sorry Topaz, I didn't see you," said Lindie Lou.

"It's okay," said Topaz. "I'm trying to find the center. It's a big open area in the middle. When we reach it, we'll be halfway through."

"Have you been in this maze before?" asked Lindie Lou.

"Sure," replied Topaz. "I know it's here somewhere."

Lindie Lou followed Topaz up a path and around a corner. The path ended at a wall of cornstalks.

"Not this way," barked Topaz. He shook his head. Topaz and Lindie Lou turned around and ran back the other way.

"Now where?" asked Lindie Lou.

"I'm not sure," replied Topaz. "But I know this for sure, half the fun is getting lost!"

"Agreed," barked Lindie Lou. "Let's go this way."

Without thinking, Lindie Lou ran to the right. Topaz followed. Then they ran to the left. They **ran** and **ran** some more.

"This is fun," barked Lindie Lou.

"It sure is," replied Topaz. "Let's see if we can find Jasper."

"Hey Jasper," barked Lindie Lou.

They listened.

"Jas---per," barked Topaz. They listened again.

"Over here," barked Jasper. "Come over here. I think I found something."

Topaz and Lindie Lou ran in the direction of Jasper's voice. They went around a few turns until they came to a

large open area

in the middle of the field.

Jasper was waiting for them.

"This must be the center," barked Jasper.

Topaz and Lindie Lou looked around.

"It is," replied Topaz.

"Hey Topaz, how come I found the center before you did? Haven't you been here before?"

"Yes," replied Topaz. "But mazes are tricky. The paths all look the same. Even to me."

Lindie Lou walked to the edge of the open area. She followed the cornstalks. She walked around in a circle, then sat down in the middle.

"I think the center is shaped like a pumpkin," said Lindie Lou.

Jasper and Topaz looked around.

"It's round like a pumpkin," said Topaz.

"Look over there," said Jasper. He

pointed to the top end of the large circle. There was a small, curved path with a flat edge.

"That must be the stem."

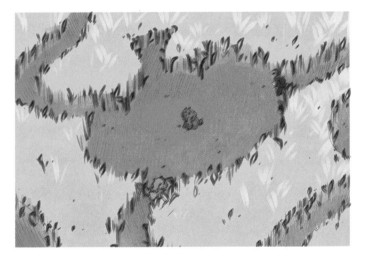

"It IS a pumpkin," barked Jasper.

"Cool," said Topaz. "Okay, now that we figured out the center, let's play a game."

"I have a great idea," said Jasper. He turned and ran down one of the paths. Jasper called over his shoulder. "Last one out of the maze has to give their treats to the others for a whole day."

"I want the treats," barked Topaz. He looked at Lindie Lou, smiled, and DISAPPEARED around a corner.

Lindie Lou stood there looking around.

I want the treats too, she thought. *I'll try this path. I think it leads to the other side of the maze. The exit must be on the other side.*

Lindie Lou walked around several

turns. The sun was moving across the sky. She noticed shadows on the path. Lindie Lou picked up her pace. She walked a long way, then she stopped and looked around.

Lindie Lou...

WAS

LOST

AGAIN!

Chapter 10

THE MAZE GAME

I'm lost, thought Lindie Lou. *If I'm going to be the first one out of this maze, I'd better find my way out FAST.*

Lindie Lou looked to the right and then to the left. Then she looked up at the sky. *I don't know what to do,* thought Lindie Lou.

Then Lindie Lou heard a sound. It was Molly. She was barking.

Lindie Lou turned toward the sound.

Molly told me she was going to find the exit and wait for us there, thought Lindie Lou. *So if I pick a path that leads me toward the sound of her bark, I should be able to find her, and the exit!*

Molly barked again.

Molly must be worried about us, thought Lindie Lou. *But she's going to confuse Topaz and Jasper because they think she's at the entrance.*

Lindie Lou thought for a moment.

First, I better find my way out. Then, if Topaz and Jasper are still in the maze I can go back in, and help them.

Lindie Lou walked in the direction of Molly's voice. The path curved around and took her the wrong way.

How am I going to figure out which way to go? thought Lindie Lou. *There are so many twists and turns in this maze.*

Lindie Lou walked a little farther. There were two trails in front of her. Neither of them led in the direction of Molly's barks. She didn't know which one to take. Lindie Lou sat down and thought for a few seconds.

Then she **Looked** up at the sky.

The sun is on the right side of the sky, thought Lindie Lou. *Molly's barks were coming from the right side too. So... if I go to the right and follow the sun, I should be able to find the exit.*

Lindie Lou smiled and picked one of the paths. It curved to the left and then to the right. The path was following the sun.

Now I know I'm going the right way, thought Lindie Lou. She smiled and kept walking.

While walking down one of the paths, Lindie Lou heard the sound of leaves crunching. She 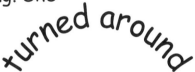 just in time to see Jasper running toward her.

"Watch out,"

barked Jasper. He ran right past Lindie Lou. Then he disappeared to the left.

Jasper was running so fast, dirt flew up from under his paws.

He just went the wrong way, thought Lindie Lou. She stopped for a minute. Lindie Lou shook her head and looked down the path. *It's too late to warn him, he's already gone.*

Lindie Lou kept walking. She followed the path for a long time.

Will I ever find my way out of here? wondered Lindie Lou.

In front of her was a beam of light. It was shining through the cornstalks. Lindie Lou ran around two more turns, then she stopped. She couldn't believe her eyes. She saw Molly, sitting on the grass, near the exit.

"There you are,"

barked Molly.

Lindie Lou ran out of the maze and over to Molly.

"What took you so long?" asked Molly. "I was worried about you." Molly hugged Lindie Lou, then she looked back into the maze. "Where are Jasper and Topaz?"

"I saw Jasper a few minutes ago," replied Lindie Lou. "He was running in the wrong direction."

Molly looked worried.

"He was running so fast, I didn't get a chance to talk to him."

Lindie Lou sat down next to Molly. They heard sounds coming from inside the maze. It sounded like crunching leaves and rustling cornstalks.

"They sound really far away," said Lindie Lou.

Molly nodded.

"Do you think
they'll
ever
find the
exit?"

Chapter 11

A-MAZE-ING

"I'm sure Topaz and Jasper will find the exit. They're smart boys," said Molly.

"I guess I won the game," said Lindie Lou.

"What game?" asked Molly.

"The last one out of the maze has to give up their treats to the other two for a whole day."

"Then you won a very nice prize," said Molly.

A little while later Topaz came **running** out of the maze. When he saw Lindie Lou and Molly, he dropped down on the ground next to them.

"I'm beat," said Topaz. "I thought I knew my way around that maze, but I kept getting lost. This cornfield is bigger than I remember."

Topaz looked around. "Where's Jasper?"

"Jasper ran past me a long time ago," replied Lindie Lou. "I think he was heading in the wrong direction."

Topaz looked at Lindie Lou.

"Then we're the first ones out and we won the game!"

"Yes," replied Lindie Lou.

Topaz rolled on his back and **RUBBED** his belly.

"I can **taste** those treats already," said Topaz. He licked his lips and sighed.

"Hey, wait a minute." Topaz rolled over and looked at Lindie Lou. "How did you find your way out before me? I thought I was in front of you?"

"Let's just say... I had a little help," replied Lindie Lou.

I learned this life lesson all by myself, thought Lindie Lou.

"What kind of help?" asked Topaz.

"When I felt lost and didn't know which way to go...

I stopped, listened for sounds, and followed the sun."

Topaz looked at Molly, then he looked up at the sky.

"Brilliant," he replied.

"I think we'd better look for Jasper," said Molly. "He should have been out by now."

"I think I should go back in and look for him," said Lindie Lou.

"Maybe I should bark," said Molly.

"If Jasper hears you bark, he might

think you're at the entrance," replied Lindie Lou.

"I have an idea," said Topaz. "Let's **ALL** bark and see if he can hear us."

"Okay," replied Lindie Lou.

Topaz, Molly, and Lindie Lou started to bark.

They waited and listened. There was no reply.

A few seconds later, they barked again. This time they heard a bark coming from deep inside the maze. They barked again and listened. The bark was closer this time.

"It's Jasper," said Molly.

Lindie Lou, Molly, and Topaz kept barking. They **barked** and **barked**. Each time Jasper's reply sounded much closer.

"He's almost here," said Lindie Lou.

"He's going to be surprised when he finds out he's the last one out," said Topaz, "because he ran faster than both of us."

They listened again. This time they heard the sound of cornstalks crackling.

"Here I come," yelled Jasper.

"Get out of the way!"

Jasper came

crashing

through a wall of cornstalks. He was running so fast he couldn't stop. Leaves and branches were flying everywhere. Lindie Lou jumped out of the way. Jasper almost ran her over.

"Jasper, be careful," barked Molly.

"I'm sorry," replied Jasper. He fell to the ground.

Jasper was panting so hard his whole body **shook.**

"Look at the hole you made in the corn maze," barked Topaz.

They all looked at the maze. There was a big hole right next to the exit.

"Well, I almost found the exit," barked Jasper.

"Okay," replied Lindie Lou. "Game over. Let's go get our **treats.**"

"Jasper, we get yours," barked Topaz, "for a whole day."

"I know," replied Jasper, "but I can beat you all at the...

Sliding game."

"That's true," said Lindie Lou.

Topaz, Lindie Lou, Jasper, and Molly turned away from the cornfield and walked toward Mark and Patty's house.

"Today was a-maze-ing," joked Lindie Lou. She nudged Topaz.

"That's corn-y," replied Topaz. He poked Jasper.

"Oh, grow up," barked Jasper.

Molly rolled her eyes.

Chapter 12

AN ORGANIC FARM

The next morning, Lindie Lou was sound asleep in the hayloft. Topaz and Jasper were sleeping next to her. Lindie Lou opened her eyes, stretched out her huge front paws and arched her back. She turned to look at the morning light. The sun was streaming in through the window.

Lindie Lou climbed out of her bed and walked over to the edge of the hayloft.

Bryan was standing near the barn door, looking at a map.

"It's a great day to go kayaking," said Bryan. "Kate are you ready?"

"Here I come," replied Kate.

"The Raccoon River is about a fifteen-minute drive," said Bryan. "The kayaks we rented will be waiting at the water's edge."

"Great," replied Kate. "Let's go."

Lindie Lou watched Bryan and Kate leave the barn. They jumped into a car and drove away. Lindie Lou was about to fall asleep again when Ronda walked into the barn.

"Wake up, puppies," she called. "I made breakfast for you. Come and eat."

Lindie Lou **loved** to eat. She jumped up and ran down the stairs. Topaz and Jasper lifted their heads, stretched a little, and followed Lindie Lou.

Ronda led the puppies into the house. Three bowls of food were sitting on the floor.

"Sit," said Ronda. All three puppies sat in front of her.

"Good," she said. "Wait," Ronda stepped back, holding up her hand. Then she said, "Okay."

Lindie Lou, Topaz, and Jasper ran to their bowls.

This food tastes great, thought Lindie Lou. *It's fresh and it's crisp. It must have come from someone's garden.*

When they were finished, Ronda opened the back door.

"Let's go for a ride," she said.

Lindie Lou was the first puppy out the door. Ronda was still in the kitchen. Lindie Lou turned and saw Ronda through the open door. She was stuffing treats into her pockets.

"Hey, Topaz," barked Lindie Lou. "Today is the day we get Jasper's treats."

Lindie Lou and Topaz licked their lips. Jasper shook his head.

Ronda came out of her house, walked over to the van, and opened the back door. She helped the puppies inside. There were enough seats for each of them to sit near a window.

"We're going to Curt and Angie's organic farm today," said to Ronda.

Ronda drove down the road. Farmers were in the fields. They were harvesting crops. Ronda knew everyone. She waved as she drove by.

"Look at those big machines," said Jasper.

"They're called combines," replied Topaz.

"There sure are a lot of them," barked Lindie Lou.

"It's harvest time," replied Topaz. "This is the time of year when farmers gather bulk crops, store them, then sell them during the year."

Ronda drove up Curt and Angie's driveway. She **beeped** her horn, then parked. Angie came running over to the van. Five of her twelve children followed.

Ronda jumped out and hugged everyone. She opened the back door and all the puppies jumped out too.

The children ran over to pet the puppies. Ronda counted the children.

"One, two, three, four, five. Where are the rest?"

"The other seven are at school," replied Angie."

"Of course they are," said Ronda. She looked around. "Where are Joe and Sherry?"

"They're in the garden picking vegetables," replied Angie. "Curt is with them."

"Okay everyone, let's go see what they're picking," said Ronda.

"This way," said Angie.

Ronda and Angie walked toward the back of the house. The children and the puppies ran ahead of them.

Rows of vegetables grew in straight lines. Curt, Joe, and Sherry were picking vegetables and putting them into a wagon.

"Our customers will be very happy with our yield this year," said Curt.

"Look what I found," said Sherry.

She pulled a **giant** carrot out of the ground.

"That is the biggest carrot I've ever seen," replied Joe. "The soil must be very good."

"It is," replied Curt. "It's organic soil. It's a mix of last year's plants and this year's animal waste."

"You mean poop," said Ronda.

Curt turned and looked at Ronda.

"Yes, I mean poop, Ronda."

The children giggled.

"Well, if poop grows vegetables like these, then it's a good thing," said Joe. "I'm sure you wash them very well."

"We do," replied Angie.

"Earthworms are good too," said Curt. "They dig tunnels in the soil, letting air and water get to the roots of the plants."

One of the boys pulled a worm out of the dirt and threw it at his sister. She screamed and ran away.

"We're a certified organic farm,"

said Angie. "We don't use any chemicals or pest control on our plants." She picked a ripe red tomato and put it in the wagon.

"Then how do you control the bugs?" asked Ronda. She snickered and looked at the children.

"Bugs, bugs, bugs," sang the children. They pretended their fingers were bugs and tickled each other.

"Actually, we MANAGE our bugs," replied Curt. "We allow them to eat part of our crops. It's a healthy way to grow food."

"The damaged crops aren't thrown

away," said Angie. "They're used to feed animals and to make fertilizer."

"Sounds like a wise farming plan," said Joe.

"Can we help you pick?" asked Ronda.

"Sure," replied Curt. "Here are some gloves. We're picking extra today. We're supplying the food for the

harvest party

tomorrow night."

Everyone joined in. They talked about tomorrow's events, while they picked ripe vegetables.

Topaz looked around. He had another idea.

"Hey, Lindie Lou and Jasper, follow me," he barked.

Chapter 13

WHAT'S IN THERE?

Lindie Lou and Jasper followed Topaz away from the organic garden.

"I know they're here somewhere," whispered Topaz.

"What?" asked Lindie Lou.

"Be quiet," replied Topaz. "You'll scare them."

"Scare who?" asked Jasper.

"Just be quiet and follow me. I'll show you."

Topaz led Lindie Lou and Jasper down

the driveway and toward the front of Curt and Angie's house.

"They're over here."

Topaz walked across the front lawn and over to the other side of the house.

"There they are," whispered Topaz.

Lindie Lou and Jasper didn't see anything. All they saw was a large shed.

"Be very quiet," said Topaz. "You don't want to scare them."

"Scare who?" asked Jasper.

"Shhhhh. Follow me," replied Topaz. He tiptoed up to the door of the shed, pushed it open with his nose, and slid inside. Lindie Lou and Jasper followed him.

"I don't see anything except another door," whispered Lindie Lou.

"Not for long," replied Topaz. He walked a little farther and jumped up on the second door. It swung open and a group of silkie chickens

scattered

in every direction.

"Let's have some fun," barked Topaz. He chased one of the chickens around the room. Jasper chased one too.

The chickens scurried everywhere. They ran all over the coop. Each one tried to outrun the one in front of it.

Topaz was about to catch one of the gray chickens, when it flew up in the air and landed on a wooden ledge.

The chickens ran so fast, some of their feathers fell out. A bunch of them landed near Lindie Lou. They tickled her nose and made her sneeze.

"Hey, Lindie Lou," barked Topaz. "Catch the white one. It's coming right at you."

A white silkie ran toward Lindie Lou. She jumped up, grabbed it with her

huge front paws, and pushed it into a corner.

"You got it," barked Topaz.

The chicken was so scared it squawked and squealed and screeched.

The noise was so loud it hurt Lindie Lou's ears. She backed away and let it go. The chicken flapped its wings and flew up on the wooden ledge.

The chickens were looking down at the puppies. They were squawking and scolding them.

"That was fun," barked Topaz. He smiled at Lindie Lou.

Lindie Lou **shuddered.**

"If I could fly, I'd catch one right now," said Jasper. He jumped up, but the chickens were too high. Jasper landed on the ground near Topaz.

"Hey, I almost caught one," barked Topaz.

"WHAT IN THE WORLD DO YOU THINK YOU'RE DOING IN HERE?" yelled Ronda. She rushed into the chicken coop and looked at the **mess.**

"Uh-oh," barked Topaz. "Follow me."

Topaz ran toward the back of the chicken coop, pushed a door open, and ran outside. Lindie Lou and Jasper followed him.

Ronda ran to the door. "No treats for you today!" she scolded.

The puppies ran up the back lawn, past the barn, and hid behind the silo.

"Thanks a lot," barked Jasper. "Now we've lost our treats from Ronda."

"Sorry," replied Topaz, "but wasn't it worth it?"

Lindie Lou shook her head.

"There's a life lesson here," she said. **"When we do something we're not supposed to, we might get punished."**

"Hey, I have another surprise for you," said Topaz.

"No more surprises," said Lindie Lou.

"But this one is really special."

"What?" asked Jasper.

"Come meet another neighbor," said Topaz. "She lives next door."

"Why should we meet her?" asked Jasper.

"Because Vicki makes the best food I've ever eaten and she gives me samples every time I visit."

"Okay," barked Lindie Lou. "At least we'll get some **treats** today."

"I'm not going," said Jasper. He put his head down, turned, and walked away.

Topaz looked at Lindie Lou.

"Even though Jasper lost the game,

maybe we should let him have some of Vicki's treats," said Topaz.

"I'd like Jasper to come with us," said Lindie Lou. "So it's okay with me."

Jasper turned and looked at Topaz and Lindie Lou.

"Then follow me," said Topaz.

Topaz lifted his nose and his tail in the air and walked toward the house next door. Lindie Lou and Jasper followed.

Chapter 14

I SEE YOU BROUGHT
SOME FRIENDS

Lindie Lou and Jasper followed Topaz down the driveway and onto the side of the road. They turned left and walked past a **huge** cornfield.

"Your neighbor surely grows a lot of corn," said Jasper.

"It looks like they grow enough to feed the **whole world**," said Lindie Lou.

"They do their part," replied Topaz. "I see truckloads of crops leaving these fields every fall during the harvest."

Topaz turned and walked up the next driveway. He lifted his nose and sniffed the air.

"Vicki must be baking," said Topaz. "I can smell her cooking all the way out here."

"It smells better than the chicken coop, that's for sure," said Jasper.

All three puppies walked up the stairs to Vicki and Mike's front door. Topaz **scratched** on the door.

"Is that you, Topaz?" came a voice from inside the house.

"I told you she knew me," barked Topaz.

A lady opened the front door. She looked out and smiled.

"Hi, Topaz. I see you brought some friends with you. Hmm, let me guess." She pointed at Jasper. "You're the **black**-and-white puppy. You must belong to Joe and Sherry, so your name is Jasper." Jasper wagged his tail. "You must be Lindie Lou," she said. "Ronda told me about your **big** paws." Lindie Lou sat up on her hind legs and flopped her big paws in front of her.

"Well, come on in," said Vicki. She opened the door and the puppies followed her into the kitchen. A dozen freshly made pumpkin pies were sitting on the kitchen table.

"I made these pies for the harvest party tomorrow night," said Vicki. She picked up one of the pies and showed it to the puppies. "I used my award-winning recipe to make this one. It's a pumpkin cheesecake pie."

Vicki set it down. Then she held up another pie. "This one is made from a new recipe I tried. It's a pumpkin pie with chocolate drizzled on top. I call it my muddy pumkey." She proudly showed the pie to the puppies. *They licked their lips.*

"Would you like to try some pumpkin dog treats?" asked Vicki.

The puppies jumped up on Vicki's legs. They were all smiling at her.

"Okay, sit," said Vicki.

Vicki went around the table and over to the kitchen counter.

"Here they are," she said. Vicki gave each one of the puppies two doggie treats. They ate them quickly, then **LOOKED UP** and begged for more.

"I'm glad you like my treats," said

Vicki. She gave them each one more. "These pies need time to cool. Let's go see what my husband Mike is up to."

The puppies followed Vicki out of the house and into the backyard. Behind the house there was another huge cornfield and a large pumpkin patch.

"Hey, Mike," called Vicki.

Mike was sitting on a tractor. He drove over to Vicki. In the back of the tractor was a wagon loaded with pumpkins.

"Do you think I have enough?" asked Mike. He looked over his shoulder.

Vicki walked over and counted the pumpkins.

"Yes, you have plenty," said Vicki. "Can you please take them over to the barn? People are going to start showing up soon."

"Okay," replied Mike. He drove the tractor over to their barn, opened the door, and drove inside.

Lindie Lou heard a sound coming from the front of the house.

BEEP BEEP

Ronda's van pulled up and stopped near Vicki.

"We're here," called Ronda.

Six more cars pulled up behind the van. Ronda opened the doors and her friends jumped out. Parents with children poured out of the other cars.

The children ran up to Vicki with their arms open. She bent down and gave each one of them a **big hug**.

"Welcome, everyone," said Vicki. "Looks like we have enough people to carve the pumpkins."

"Okay, let's get to it," said Ronda.

Everyone followed Vicki into the barn.

Chapter 15

PUMPKIN CARVING

The inside of Mike and Vicki's barn was empty, except for some straw scattered on the floor, and several bales of hay stored up in the rafters.

Mike lifted the pumpkins out of the wagon and placed them on long wooden tables, arranged in a square pattern.

"Come on in," sang Vicki.

Joe and Sherry walked in first. Jasper followed. Then came Curt and Angie. All twelve of their children ran behind them. Ronda and Patty came in together. Topaz and Lindie Lou followed Ronda. Behind Ronda were the rest of their friends.

"Patty, where's your husband, Mark?" asked Vicki. "He loves carving **PUMPKINS**."

"He's out harvesting soybeans," replied Patty.

"When Mike is finished unloading the rest of the pumpkins, he's going out to harvest our fields too," replied Vicki.

"Where are Kate and Bryan?"

"They went kayaking on the Raccoon River," said Ronda. "I hope they make it back in time to carve a pumpkin."

Vicki walked to the middle of the room.

"Welcome, everyone. Please pick a pumpkin. Keep in mind that the candles in these pumpkins will be our only source of light for the harvest party tomorrow night. So, carve them wisely."

"Okay," replied the guests.

"Looks like we got here just in time," said Bryan to Kate. They walked over to Ronda. Lindie Lou ran to greet them. Kate picked Lindie Lou up and gave her a **big hug.**

"Hi, Kate and Bryan. I'm Vicki, and this is my husband, Mike. It's nice to meet you." They all shook hands. "Help yourselves to a pumpkin."

"I like this shape," said Kate. She picked a **tall, skinny** one.

"This one is really cool," said Bryan. He picked a short, flat pumpkin.

"I'd like to carve the big one over there," said Sherry. She wrapped her arms around a pumpkin the size of a

BEACH BALL.

"I like the color of this pumpkin," said Joe. He picked a green-and-yellow striped one.

Lindie Lou and Jasper walked over to Topaz.

"We aren't going to find any food in here," said Topaz, "unless you want to eat pumpkin guts."

"Yuck," replied Lindie Lou.

"I'm still hungry," said Topaz. "Let's go see if we can find a way to get back into Vicki's kitchen."

"Great idea," said Jasper. "I can't stop thinking about those pies."

Topaz, Jasper, and Lindie Lou walked toward the house.

"Wait a minute," said Lindie Lou. "Vicki's pies are for the harvest party."

"We won't eat them all," said Topaz.

"Right," said Jasper. "We'll leave some for tomorrow night's party."

Lindie Lou stopped.

"Well, I'm not going with you. Vicki worked all day making those pies for the party and I'm not going to eat them."

"More pie for us," said Topaz.

"Let's go," said Jasper.

Lindie Lou turned and walked away from Topaz and Jasper. She walked to the end of Mike and Vicki's driveway. Across the street was a soybean field.

The last time I was in a soybean field I had a lot of fun, thought Lindie Lou. *This time I'll make sure I don't get lost. I'll use the sun to find my way out.*

Lindie Lou

at the sky. The afternoon sun was on her right. She looked back at the barn.

No one will miss me, she thought. *Everyone is busy carving pumpkins.*

Lindie Lou crossed the street and walked into the soybean field. The plants swept against her fur. It reminded her of being brushed by Kate after a bath.

Lindie Lou looked up at the sky. The sun was easy to see. She knew exactly where she was and how to get back to Mike and Vicki's farm. Lindie Lou kept walking.

A little while later, she saw a gray mouse run by. Lindie Lou decided to chase it.

I won't catch it. I'll just chase it, thought Lindie Lou.

Lindie Lou chased the mouse. It ran back and forth. Then it ran in a

Lindie Lou ran as fast as she could. The mouse ran faster. The faster the

mouse ran, the faster Lindie Lou ran. The mouse tried to get away. It started running in smaller circles. Lindie Lou kept chasing it. She noticed that her back foot was getting tangled in the soybean plants, but she kept running until she couldn't move.

Her foot was all wrapped up in soybean plants. She tried to pull it out

but it was too tangled.

Lindie Lou yanked and pulled, but the more she moved, the tighter the plants wrapped around her foot.

Then, Lindie Lou heard a

loud, thrashing

sound.

Something very big, was moving toward her!

Chapter 16

WHAT AM I GOING TO DO?

The sound was coming closer and the ground around Lindie Lou started to **RUMBLE.**

Lindie Lou didn't know what to do. She started barking, but no one heard her. Everyone was in the barn carving pumpkins. Even Molly was far away. She was back at Ronda's house resting up before the harvest party.

Topaz and Jasper couldn't hear her either. They were at Vicki and Mike's house trying to get inside to eat her pies.

Lindie Lou couldn't see what was coming, but she could hear it.

Dust was flying everywhere, and the noise was getting closer. She tried to pull her foot free, but it was too tangled.

What am I going to do?

Lindie Lou saw several field mice run by. They were running away from the noise.

Lindie Lou looked up. She could finally see where the noise was coming from. The mice were running away from a COMBINE.

It had giant rotating blades and was moving down the field. It was pulling soybean plants out of the ground, squeezing the beans out. Then, it threw the beans into a grain tank behind the combine and blew the leftover pods back into the field.

I'm doomed,

thought Lindie Lou. She kept trying to free her foot.

"RUN," came a voice from behind Lindie Lou.

"FASTER," said another voice.

Topaz came roaring through the soybean field. He ran right over the top of Lindie Lou. Jasper was behind him. He banged into Topaz.

"Lindie Lou, what are you doing here?" asked Topaz. "THE COMBINE IS COMING."

"I'M STUCK," yelled Lindie Lou.

Topaz and Jasper looked at Lindie Lou's foot.

"CHEW," yelled Jasper.

Topaz and Jasper started chewing at the plants wrapped around Lindie Lou's foot.

Lindie Lou looked up at the combine. It was getting closer.

"EVERYONE LOOK OUT,"

barked Lindie Lou. "The combine is coming!"

Jasper and Topaz darted to the other side of Lindie Lou.

The combine rumbled past them.

All three puppies were shook up, but they were not hurt.

"You saved our lives," said Topaz.

"Yeah, thanks," said Jasper.

"We still have to get you out of here," said Topaz.

Jasper and Topaz started chewing and pulling on the plants around Lindie Lou's foot. Lindie Lou listened. The combine was still in the field.

"I don't think we have much time," said Lindie Lou.

"LET'S LOOK."

All three puppies stuck their heads out of the field and looked down the newly cut path.

The combine was turning around.

"It's coming back!" said Lindie Lou, and this time it's coming right at us!"

"And you're still stuck!" barked Jasper.

"DIG," yelled Topaz.

Jasper and Topaz started digging. They dug as fast as they could.

Lindie Lou pulled as hard as she could. Her brothers kept digging. The roots of the plants started to loosen. Just when the combine was getting too close, the plants around Lindie Lou's foot came loose. The puppies rolled out of the way,

JUST IN TIME.

The combine rumbled past them, again.

Lindie Lou, Topaz, and Jasper looked at each other. They were all covered with dust and dried leaves.

"Lindie Lou, you look like a pile of dirt," said Topaz. "All I can see are your eyes."

"So do you," barked Jasper.

Lindie Lou **shook** the dust and leaves off her fur. So did Topaz and Jasper.

"Let's get out of here before the combine comes back," said Lindie Lou.

The puppies ran out of the field.

"Is your foot okay?" asked Jasper.

"Yes, thanks," replied Lindie Lou. She looked at Topaz. "This time YOU saved my life," said Lindie Lou.

"Now we're even," barked Topaz.

Jasper nodded.

"By the way," said Lindie Lou. "Why were you two in the field?"

"We couldn't get into Vicki and Mike's house," said Topaz.

"Right," said Jasper. "So we didn't eat any pies."

"Oh, good," said Lindie Lou.

"So we decided to chase some mice," said Topaz.

"I'm glad you were out here," said Lindie Lou.

"We are too," said Topaz.

"In the future, Lindie Lou, please be more careful," said Jasper. "We might not be around the next time you get in trouble."

"Okay," replied Lindie Lou.

"Hey, I hear someone coming," said Topaz.

"There you are,"

said Kate. "I'm glad I have this tracking device with me." She held up a small, square, plastic gizmo.

Lindie Lou ran up to Kate. Topaz and Jasper followed. Kate saw the combine rumbling through the field.

"You puppies aren't supposed to be out here all by yourselves. You could get seriously injured. **Next time, make sure you let an adult know where you're going before you go off on your own,**" said Kate. "And you're covered in dirt!" She shook her head. "Come on, follow me. I'm going to have to give you all a bath before tomorrow's harvest party."

Chapter 17

THE HARVEST DAY PARADE

Lindie Lou woke up very early. She was excited because today was

HARVEST DAY.

This was the day farmers celebrated their fall harvest.

Lindie Lou looked over at Topaz and Jasper. They were sound asleep. She stretched out her big front paws and stood up.

Lindie Lou heard Kate say to Bryan... "The Harvest Day Parade begins at noon. We still have plenty of time to eat breakfast with Pete and Ronda."

"Great," replied Bryan.

Lindie Lou ran down from the hayloft.

"Good morning girl," said Bryan. "Are you hungry?"

Topaz and Jasper's heads popped up. They ran down the stairs too. All three puppies wagged their tails.

"Follow us," said Kate.

After breakfast Ronda led everyone to her bright-purple van.

"The Party Barge is ready to roll," said Ronda.

Angie, Curt, and their twelve children were already at the parade. They were sitting on the curb saving places for the rest of their group. Ronda had told them to sit in front of

T&D's Cafe.

Ronda loved the taste of their cinnamon-spiced pumpkin soup, which they served every year during the parade.

"Come sit with me Lindie Lou," said one of the children named Emmy. Lindie Lou sat down next to Emmy. "You're my favorite puppy," she said. Emmy put her arm around Lindie Lou.

"Jasper, come sit on this side of me," said Krystal, "and Topaz can sit on my other side." She petted Topaz's head.

"Good," said her sister Bridget, "then Topaz will be in front of me."

"And Jasper will be sitting next to me," said her brother Lee.

Emmy Danni   Lee   Ryan Krystal Bridget Rayce
  Lindie Lou   Jasper   Topaz

Lindie Lou had never been to a parade before. She looked around. The grown-ups were sitting in chairs behind the children and the puppies.

"Hey, Mom and Dad," said a boy named Rayce, who was sitting next to Topaz. "Here come the **police** cars."

"Then the parade is about to begin," said Angie. She tapped her son Rayce on the head.

"Look, behind the police cars," said Lee. "Here comes the first band."

Danni was sitting behind Emmy.

"Hey Mom, look. Some of the band

members are playing trumpets." Danni looked up at her mom. "I'll be in the parade next year playing my trumpet."

"I can't wait," said Angie. She leaned over and put her hand on Danni's shoulder.

The band marched by, playing...

"AMERICA THE BEAUTIFUL."

Everyone stood up and sang along. They sang the words...

"AMBER WAVES OF GRAIN"

louder than any of the other words.

Many colorful floats passed by. One of them was covered with cornstalks and sunflowers. A group of teenagers were dressed like scarecrows. They danced and waved at the crowd.

Another float had bundles of wheat stalks sitting in brightly colored pots. A woman was standing in front of an oven. She was showing the crowd a tray of freshly baked muffins.

Music could be heard from another marching band. They played the

"STAR SPANGLED BANNER."

The next float carried the annual Harvest Queen. She was sitting on top of several bales of hay. The runners-up sat next to her. They all waved gently to the crowd. Everyone clapped and waved back.

Next came the mayor, Joe Seedling and his wife, Sue. They waved from the back of a **bright-red** convertible.

In the car behind them was a man from India. He was the winner of this year's World Food Prize. He developed a way to grow healthier wheat crops.

"Look, here come the cows," said a little girl named Mandy.

Mark walked by with six of his **ANGUS cattle.**

Pete and Mike helped keep them in line. The cattle wore *brass bells that jingled* around their necks.

Patty, Ronda, and Vicki stood up and cheered.

"Hey, Mark, where's your prize bull?" yelled Ronda.

"Probably looking for your Party Barge," laughed Mark.

Ronda smiled and gave Mark the thumbs-up signal.

"Look what's behind the cows," said Curt and Angie's son, Ryan. He was wearing a **Cub Scout** uniform.

"What?" asked Ronda. She looked over Ryan's shoulder.

"PUMPKINS," said Ryan.

"My favorite part," said Ronda. She put her hand on Ryan's shoulder.

"Mine too," said Ryan.

Four tractors rolled by, each pulling a trailer. Giant pumpkins with ribbons on them passed by.

"That pumpkin is huge," said Kate.

"It's the size of a **humongous** bean bag chair," said Angie.

"The next pumpkin is as big as a boulder," said Bryan.

"Look at the one behind it. It's shaped like a giant banana," said Patty.

Everyone laughed.

"Here comes the biggest one of all," said Ryan. He stood up to get a better look.

"What we have here, is this year's winner of the...

World's Largest Pumpkin Award,"

said the parade marshal over a loudspeaker. "It's Dick and Catherine Treeker's pumpkin. They brought it all the way from Sheboygan, Wisconsin. Their pumpkin weighed in at a record-breaking 2,126 pounds."

The Treekers were on a trailer with their winning pumpkin. Mrs. Treeker waved to the crowd. Everyone clapped and cheered.

"The winning pumpkin is... white," said Curt and Angie's daughter Libby. "Can a real pumpkin be white?"

"Pumpkins are many colors," said Sherry. "Joe carved a

green-and-yellow

striped one yesterday."

The next float held even more pumpkins. They all had ribbons on them too. A family dressed in farm clothes danced on the float. They reached into plastic pumpkin buckets, grabbed handfuls of candy, and tossed the candy to the children.

Krystal caught a small bag of candy corn.

"This is MY favorite part," said Mandy. She caught a small bag of

Jelly beans.

"The horses are coming," called Bridget. "Look, they're dancing!"

A group of marching horses pranced by. Their riders wore colorful, leather-fringed, costumes. The horses danced in circles. Some walked sideways. A few even walked backwards.

Curt reached for Angie's hand.

"We had another good harvest," he said.

"We sure did," said Angie. She smiled and squeezed his hand.

"There's the last police car," said Ronda. She stood up and waved at the officers.

"The parade must be over," said Vicki.

Ronda turned to her friends and family. "Okay, everyone, it's time to get ready for the harvest party. I'll see you at Curt and Angie's barn later tonight."

"Ronda, I can hardly wait to see your costume," said Sherry.

"I promise, it won't disappoint," smiled Ronda.

"I'm sure it won't," said Bryan.

Ronda grinned, clapped her hands, and jumped up and down.

Chapter 18

THE HARVEST PARTY

Later that evening, family, friends, and neighbors arrived at Curt and Angie's barn.

Curt and Angie were still in the house. They were helping their children get into costumes. Vicki and Mike agreed to meet and greet the guests.

"We can open the doors as soon as Kate and Bryan give us the signal," said Vicki. "They're inside lighting candles."

A little while later, a cow bell...

 jingled.

"There's the signal," said Mike. He opened the barn doors.

"Come on in, everyone," said Vicki. She led the guests into the barn. Everyone looked around. They were amazed at what they saw.

The barn was transformed into a magical celebration of the harvest. There were cornstalks covering the walls. Bales of HAY were stacked in the corners, and up in the rafters.

Scarecrows could be seen around the room. Some were waving; one looked as if it were dancing. One was standing very straight with a crow sitting on its shoulder.

Candles flickered inside the carved pumpkins, which Mike brought over, earlier that day. They gave the room a golden glow. On the ceiling was a cluster of white puffy clouds.

Silver glitter lined their edges. The clouds twinkled in the candlelight.

A **bright-red** barn was built for the children to play in. On two sides of

the room were long tables full of wonderful, colorful, amazing-smelling food.

"Vicki was up most of the night preparing our harvest party meal," said Mike. He led the guests over to the food tables.

There were soups made from pumpkins and butternut squash. Carrots and celery were offered, with a dipping sauce. The seven-layer salad was this year's favorite dish. Pizza and potato wedges were popular with the kids. Eggplant had been baked in a very big pan, and in the middle of the table sat a small scarecrow.

Vicki's pumpkin pies were sitting on

the dessert table. Large bowls of soft-serve ice cream could be scooped with a ladle. Children ran over so they could see one of the pies. It was topped with candy corn.

Guests were standing in the food line with plates in their hands. They talked and laughed and looked around.

Everyone was in costume.

Some of the guests pointed to their favorite pumpkins. Others tried to guess who was behind the masks.

Curt and Angie's children ran into the barn. They were dressed like little gray field mice. Angie and Curt waddled in next. They were dressed like silkie chickens. Curt flapped his wings. Everyone clapped and cheered.

"Hey, Mike, you make a mighty fine cornstalk," said Mark. He was dressed in a carrot costume.

"Is that you, Mark?" asked Mike. "You look very organic."

Mark flashed him two thumbs up.

"Be careful of the rabbit over there," said Mike. "She might take a **bite** out of you."

"That's Patty," laughed Mark.

"Is that you, Vicki?" asked a neighbor. "Your American goldfinch costume is amazing."

"Yes, it's me," replied Vicki. She lifted her beak and smiled. "I borrowed this costume from Ronda."

"Here comes Lindie Lou, Jasper, and Topaz," said Libby. "Look, the puppies are dressed up like a grasshopper, a ladybug, and a bumblebee."

"My costume feels strange," said Topaz. He **wiggled** his stinger.

"They were Ronda's idea," said Lindie Lou. She jiggled her antennae.

"At least you're not green," replied Jasper.

"Hey, look," said Topaz. "Someone is dressed up like you, Lindie Lou, and someone is dressed like Jasper."

"It's Kate and Bryan," said Lindie Lou. "I watched them make those costumes at our house in Seattle."

"There's our mom, Molly," said Topaz. "She's dressed up like a baby COW."

"Wow. I thought it was a REAL calf," said Jasper.

"The farmer sitting next to her must be Joe," said Lindie Lou.

"Sherry is supposed to be dressed like a haystack," said Jasper. "I watched her stick those pieces of hay in her hair."

"Hey, let's go find some food," said Topaz. "Those kids dressed up like mice are our best bet. They're eating popcorn."

"Smells yummy," said Lindie Lou.

"Look who's coming to see us," said the girl named Danni. She bent down to pet Lindie Lou. "You sure are a cute little ladybug."

The children made a circle around the puppies. They sprinkled popcorn on the floor and watched them eat.

"A popcorn party! We're having a popcorn party!" sang Danni.

Vicki walked over to a microphone.

"Welcome everyone, to this year's harvest party," she announced. "Now that everyone is finished eating, let's form a line and walk past the three judges. They will pick the **winners** of this year's costume contest."

"Should we try to win a prize?" asked Jasper.

"I'd rather eat popcorn," replied Lindie Lou.

"Me too," said Topaz.

"Let's give Curt and Angie a big round of applause for giving us food from their amazing organic garden," said Vicki.

Everyone *clapped* and **cheered**.

"And a special thanks to Mike for helping me prepare tonight's dinner and for bringing us the pumpkins."

Everyone clapped again. Someone yelled, "You rock, Vicki."

Vicki smiled and waved.

"And to everyone who helped carve pumpkins and decorate Curt and Angie's barn."

The crowd clapped and whistled.

Curt looked around the room. "Has anyone seen Ronda?" he asked.

"You'll see her soon enough," replied Pete. "She's still getting ready."

"I hope she doesn't miss the costume contest," said Angie.

Chapter 19

AND THE WINNERS ARE...

Pete walked up to Vicki. She smiled and handed him the microphone.

"Good evening everyone," said Pete. He was dressed like the mayor. "Thank you for coming to this year's harvest party. I hope everyone's having a good time."

The audience clapped. The real mayor, Joe Seedling, waved at Pete.

"It's time to announce this year's costume contest winners. Please move to the sides of the barn."

Everyone stepped back. Pete was now standing by himself in the middle of the barn.

"Lights, please," said Pete.

Mike and Mark pointed two bright spotlights on Pete.

"Now is the moment we've all been waiting for," said Pete. "Judges, would you please bring me the names of the winners."

One of the judges walked up to Pete. She took a piece of paper out of her pocket and handed it to him.

"Let's give the judges a big hand."

Everyone clapped.

The judges bowed.

Pete opened the piece of paper and cleared his throat.

"The prize for this year's funniest costumes goes to...

the fuzzy silkie chickens."

Curt and Angie waddled over to Pete. They flapped their wings, turned around, and wiggled their tail feathers.

Everyone laughed and cheered.

"Next are the winners of the most creative costumes." This year the prize goes to...

the cornstalk
and
the haystack."

Mike and Sherry walked over to Pete, jumped up and down, and accepted their ribbons.

Everyone clapped and laughed.

"And...the award for the most original costumes goes to... Kate and Bryan for their Lindie Lou and Jasper costumes."

Bryan and Kate skipped to the center of the room, opened their hoods, smiled at each other, and then waved to the crowd.

"Woohoo," howled Lindie Lou.

"Arf arf," barked Jasper.

"How come none of the costumes look like me?" asked Topaz.

"Because the kids dressed like mice, would be afraid of you," teased Jasper.

"Very funny," said Topaz. "I think I'll go over and sting them with my stinger."

Lindie Lou and Jasper held Topaz back. He growled at the kids, then looked at Lindie Lou and Jasper and snickered.

"Attention, everyone," said Pete. "It is now time to announce our grand prize winner."

The room became very quiet.

Pete looked at the judge's paper, again. Mike and Mark pointed four spotlights on Pete.

"This year's grand prize winner is…"

The room was so quiet you could hear a dog pant.

"MOTHER HARVEST."

"Mother Harvest?" asked someone in the crowd. "Who could it be?"

Pete pointed up at the clouds, bowed, and backed away from the center of the room.

The four spotlights moved up into the clouds. Their silver edges glittered in the light. The spots of light started to circle around the ceiling. Then they lit up the crowd. Everyone was smiling.

Pete lifted his arms and the lights stopped. Then they shut off. The whole room went dark, except for the candlelight flickering from inside the pumpkins.

A small flame appeared in the middle of the clouds. It lit a cluster of sparklers hanging from the ceiling.

Everyone gasped. Mike picked up a hose, just in case.

The flame from the sparklers flickered and fizzed. The sparks streamed down toward the ground. They burned out, just before they reached the floor.

"What a beautiful sight," said Bryan. He reached over and held Kate's hand.

"Wow," whispered Sherry. "It looks like a glittery waterfall." Joe put his arm around Sherry.

When all the sparklers burned out, the room was dark again.

Then came the sound of thunder. It got **louder** and **louder**. Then it stopped.

One of the spotlights turned on and moved back and forth around the room.

Three more spotlights turned on. They moved around the room.

Then all four spotlights stopped. They were pointing up at the clouds.

Chapter 20

MOTHER HARVEST

Pete's voice echoed over the loudspeaker.

"Welcome, MOTHER HARVEST. Welcome to this year's harvest party."

Sparks burst, then smoke covered the clouds. When it cleared, a woman appeared.

She was sitting on a wooden throne. The throne drifted down from the clouds. It looked as if she was floating .

The crowd *gasped*.

"She's beautiful," said Lindie Lou.

The woman was wearing a long, white dress. On her head was a wreath made from wheat stalks dusted with...

gold glitter. She held a golden pitchfork in her hand. The handle was wrapped in corn, rice, and soybeans. Her mask was made of white feathers and gold lace.

Her blonde hair was braided in four long strands, and on her lap was a basket full of sunflowers.

Thunder **rumbled** again and afterwards the room was very quiet.

Everyone watched Mother Harvest float down toward the crowd.

"I'm very proud of you," she said. "An organic farm is the perfect place to celebrate this year's harvest."

Mother Harvest waved her pitchfork in a circle.

"Farming is a very important part of our survival. It is up to us to take care of our land, our water, and our food."

Mother Harvest's throne rested gently on the floor. She stood up and walked toward the crowd.

"Aww," said the crowd. They looked around the room and whispered to each other.

"You have done well, my fellow farmers," said Mother Harvest. "You have pleased Mother Harvest."

She bowed.

Everyone clapped.

"We are honored to have you with us, Mother Harvest," said Pete. "The judges viewed your costume earlier today and chose you to be this year's GRAND PRIZE winner." He pinned a blue ribbon on her dress.

Mother Harvest smiled at Pete, then turned to the crowd.

"Look around the room, my friends. Next spring, the inside of this barn will be full of plants, growing from the floor, all the way to the ceiling. Curt and Angie are going to build an organic, vertical farm inside this barn."

Everyone clapped and cheered.

Mother Harvest handed her pitchfork and the basket of flowers to one of the judges. Her throne floated back up into the clouds.

Mother Harvest reached up and removed her mask.

"It's RONDA," said Kate.

Everyone gasped, clapped and hooted.

Ronda waived her hand in a big circle.

"Thank you everyone," she said. She turned and looked at Pete. "Okay, let's celebrate."

The music started to play.

"Ya-hoo-ee," yelled Ronda. Pete and Ronda began to *dance*.

Everyone joined them on the dance floor.

La-la-la, la-la la-la la,   la-la-la-la,   la-la-la

"Your family sure knows how to put on a party," said Bryan.

"They sure do," replied Kate.

La-la-la, la-la la-la la,   la -la -la -la, la

Bryan spun Kate around several times.

"Hey," said Topaz to Lindie Lou. "Isn't this the song Sherry sang to us when we lived together in the Puppy Playground?"

Lindie Lou,
    you are cool, and your friends,
        think you're a jewel.

"Yes," said Lindie Lou. She swayed back and forth to the music.

La-la-la, la-la la-la la, la -la -la -la, la.

"I remember it too," said Jasper. He tapped his paw to the tune.

The puppies sat and watched everyone dance for a long time.

After a while, Topaz stood up and stretched.

"I'm hungry again," he said. "Let's go see if Vicki brought some of those tasty pumpkin dog **treats** with her."

Chapter 21

I DON'T WANT TO LEAVE

The next morning Topaz and Jasper followed Lindie Lou down the stairs and into the yard.

"Do you really have to leave?" asked Topaz. "We were having so much fun."

"I saw Bryan bring out our suitcases last night," said Lindie Lou. "They must be getting ready to pack."

Lindie Lou turned around and looked at Topaz and Jasper.

"Your visit was much too short," said Topaz.

All three puppies had a sad look on their faces.

"I don't want to leave either," said Jasper.

"You mean you're leaving too?" asked Topaz.

"Last night I heard Joe talking to

Sherry. He said we have a long drive home and should leave right after breakfast."

"I guess I'd better go check on Bryan and Kate," said Lindie Lou.

"We'll go with you," said Topaz.

The puppies walked into the barn and over to Kate and Bryan's bedroom.

"Hi, Lindie Lou," said Kate. "We sure had a good time, didn't we?"

Kate was folding clothes and putting them into her suitcase. "It's too bad we have to leave so soon."

Lindie Lou looked at Jasper and Topaz. They sat down together and looked up at Kate.

Kate closed her suitcase. Bryan closed his too.

"It was great seeing Pete and Ronda again and meeting all their friends," said Bryan.

"It sure was," replied Kate. "We learned a lot about farming and organic gardening."

"Maybe we should plant an organic garden when we get home," said Bryan.

"Great idea," replied Kate.

Topaz stood up and walked toward the door. Jasper followed him. Lindie Lou stood up too.

"Don't go too far, girl," said Bryan. "We have a plane to catch."

The puppies walked back into the barn.

"What's it like flying on an airplane?" asked Jasper.

"You haven't flown yet?" asked Lindie Lou.

"No, not yet," replied Jasper.

"It's like this," said Topaz.

He ran up the stairs and jumped off the hayloft. Topaz's arms were stretched out like airplane wings. His feet were far apart. He flipped over in the air, and landed on his back.

"Is that what it's like?" asked Jasper.

"Not exactly," replied Lindie Lou.

Topaz stood up, shook the hay off his fur, and walked back to Lindie Lou and Jasper.

Lindie Lou ran up the stairs and jumped off the hayloft. Her arms were stretched far apart, her legs were together, and her toes were pointed.

When she landed Lindie Lou said **"THUD."**

Then she stood up on her hind legs, pushed off, and slid across the barn floor on her belly. Her arms were still spread out.

"Before the airplane stops, it sounds like this... **SWOOSH."**

Lindie Lou stopped, turned around, and walked back to Jasper and Topaz.

"That was cool," said Topaz.

"Yeah," replied Jasper.

"Where are you going this time?" asked Jasper.

"Home, first," replied Lindie Lou. "But I heard Bryan talking about another trip next month. I heard him say we were going to go see a Thanksgiving Day parade. He said there would be giant balloons in the parade. He also said people call the city we're going to,

'The Big Apple.' "

"Sounds yummy," said Topaz.

"Kate also talked about visiting a

huge park. She said it was right in the middle of the city."

"What fun," said Jasper.

"Lindie Lou, it's time to go," said Kate. She walked over, picked up Lindie Lou, and set her in her blue travel carrier.

"Follow me," said Bryan. He was pulling their suitcases.

Lindie Lou looked back at Topaz and Jasper.

"I miss you already," said Lindie Lou.

"Don't worry about me," said Topaz. "I have plenty of silkie chickens and mice to chase."

"Watch out for the combine," warned Lindie Lou.

"Sure thing," barked Topaz.

"'Bye Jasper," said Lindie Lou.

"'Bye Lindie Lou," replied Jasper. "I'm going back home with Joe, Sherry, and Molly. I'll be in the Puppy Playground where the box of **STUFFED** animals are."

"Promise me you won't tear the stuffing out of them," said Lindie Lou.

"I promise," replied Jasper.

"There you all are," said Ronda as she walked into the barn. "The Party Barge is ready. Pete's driving."

Ronda held her arms in the air. She looked like an airplane ready to take off. "Let's go to the airport," she said.

Joe, Sherry, and Molly walked up the driveway.

"We came to say good-bye," said Sherry.

"Have a safe trip home," said Joe.

"Thanks. You too," replied Kate. They all hugged.

Molly walked over to Lindie Lou. They rubbed noses. Kate smiled.

Bryan, Kate, and Lindie Lou climbed into the back seat of the Party Barge. The van pulled away from the farm and drove down the long country road.

First it passed Mark and Patty's farm. Then it passed Curt and Angie's farm. When it passed Vicki and Mike's farm, they were standing outside waving goodbye.

Lindie Lou looked out the window. She sighed and **closed her eyes**.

The "Lindie Lou Song" was playing on the radio.

I can't wait to-oo see where you take me.

La la la, la-la la-la la, la la la la, la.

Lindie Lou Song

Chorus 1
La-la-la,
La-la-la-la-la,
La-la-la-la,
La-la-la.

Verse 1
L-I-N-D-I-E
L-O-U spells
Lindie Lou.

Chorus 2
La-la-la,
La-la-la-la-la,
La-la-la,
La-la.

Verse 2
Lindie Lou,
you are cool,
and your friends
think you're a jewel.

Chorus 2
La-la-la,
La-la-la-la-la,
La-la-la,
La-la.

Verse 3
You are a
very lucky girl,
'cuz you've been
all over the world.

Chorus 2
La-la-la,
La-la-la-la-la,
La-la-la,
La-la.

Verse 4
I can't wait
to see,
where you
take me.

Chorus 2
La-la-la,
La-la-la-la-la,
La-la-la,
La-la.

(Pause)

Chorus 1
La-la-la,
La-la-la-la-la,
La-la-la-la,
La-la-la.

Verse 5
You are my
little Lindie Lou,
and I love you.

Chorus 2
La-la-la,
La-la-la-la-la,
La-la-la,
La-la.

Go to lindielou.com to listen to the "Lindie Lou Song."

244

Fun Facts

- Organic farming is friendly to our planet and good for all the living things on it. This is often described as *biodiversity*.

- Some of the world's largest pumpkins can be viewed during harvest time at the annual Ryan Norlan Giant Pumpkin Weigh-Off in Anamosa, Iowa. The prize winning pumpkin is featured in a parade.

- American farmers grow an average of 2.3 billion bushels of corn per year.

- The World Food Prize goes to the person who increases the quality, quantity, or availability of food in the world.

- There are sixty to eighty pods on a soybean plant.

- Many people grow organic gardens at home.

Des Moines, Iowa • Calendar

January
HOLLYWOOD IN THE HEARTLAND. Celebrate Iowa's legacy with the silver screen throughout history. See how Iowa has been portrayed on-screen in a variety of films and meet the actors.

February
IOWA POWER FARMING. The third largest farm show in the U.S. Has exhibitions from more than 800 companies.

March
CHILDREN & FAMILIES OF IOWA'S KIDSFEST. Help at-risk families in need by bringing your family out to a kid-centered festival fundraiser full of fun activities, games, and entertainment. Play on inflatables, watch stage shows and so much more.

April
ULTIMATE DINOSAURS. Learn about awesome dinosaurs and new discoveries at the Science Center of Iowa.

May
GREATER DES MOINES FARMERS MARKETS. Starting the first Saturday of May, come taste the fresh fruit and produce at the Downtown Farmers' Market.

June
DES MOINES ARTS FESTIVAL. Catch interactive arts-related activities, live music, film, and performing arts.

July
80/35 MUSIC FESTIVAL. Watch a show on stages set in the streets of Western Gateway Park. With a variety of genres and regional and local bands, 80/35 is perfect for music fans of all ages and interests.

August
IOWA STATE FAIR. It's the true heartbeat of the Midwest. Join the great celebration and salute the state's best in agriculture, industry, entertainment and achievement.

September
DES MOINES WORLD FOOD FESTIVAL. Enjoy more than fifty international food vendors, a variety of arts and crafts vendors, like music, and special cooking demonstrations and contests.

October
WORLD FOOD PRIZE. Learn from international experts and policy leaders about decisions on cutting-edge nutrition and food security issues.

ANAMOSA PUMPKIN-FEST and RYAN NORLAN GIANT PUMPKIN WEIGH-OFF. Enjoy a true Main Street Festival. Some activities include craft vendors, food booths, kids' games, one of the largest parades in all of Iowa, and of course, GIANT pumpkins!

November
LIVING HISTORY FARMS RACE. Run seven miles in the cool November weather of Central Iowa. Wade through creeks, dodge farm animals, and claw your way to the top of gullies.

December
DOWNTOWN WINTER FARMERS' MARKET. This is the perfect opportunity to stock up for holiday meals, parties, and gifts. Farmers sell a variety of locally raised products and produce; holiday wreaths, trees, and decorations are cute pieces to pick up from the festive market.

QUICK QUIZ

1. Where did Kate, Bryan and Lindie Lou stop on their way to the Sea-Tac airport?

2. What big farm machine did Bryan see from the airplane window?

3. How are silkie chickens like Lindie Lou?

4. Would you eat raw soybeans? Why or why not?

5. How does Lindie Lou find her way out of the corn maze?

6. What is Ryan's favorite part of the parade? What is yours?

7. What three things help organic gardens grow better?

8. Why was the Harvest Festival so much fun?

9. There are three clues in Chapter 21 telling where Lindie Lou is going next. Where do you think she is going?

Answers:

(9) A Thanksgiving Day parade, the Big Apple, and a huge park; New York City.
(8) Good food, dancing, costumes, and everyone worked together.
(7) Poop, earthworms, and bugs.
(6) The pumpkins.
(5) Listening for Molly and following the sun.
(4) No, only if they are cooked. Raw soybeans can make you sick.
(3) They are fuzzy, cute, and have big feet.
(2) A combine.
(1) Seattle Public Library.

Topaz Jasper Lindie Lou Ruby Diamond

I can't wait to READ where you take me!

www.lindielou.com   PINA PUBLISHING

Lindie Lou with her Brothers and Sisters

LindieLou.com/BooksShop

TEACHERS, LIBRARIANS, AND PARENTS

Enjoy the Lindie Lou Adventure Series

Lindie Lou Adventure Series books are written for kindergarten through third-grade readers.

Parents and Teachers: Children connect with the main character, an adorable puppy named Lindie Lou. She takes them on adventures and teaches them not to be afraid. As Lindie Lou gets in and out of trouble, the reader discovers many life lessons about people, places and things.

Each book includes hints about where Lindie Lou is going, a calendar of events, places to go and a quick quiz. Extra content encourages children to continue learning even when the book is finished. After reading Book One, *Flying High*, the other books in the series can be read in any order. They are not dependent on one another.

The Lindie Lou website, lindielou.com, provides additional learning tools in a user-friendly and colorful environment. The website provides pictures, videos, illustrations, games, a song, lyrics, and more. The "Lindie Lou Song" can be heard on the song page of the website. Children enjoy this upbeat tune. The lyrics and score are also on the song page.

Videos of author Jeanne Bender show her introducing Lindie Lou to young readers. In one video, the author writes a chapter of the book and encourages young viewers to follow along and develop their writing skills.

Readers who are slow to start reading enjoy the books' large text, colorful illustrations, and creative graphics. As young readers improve their reading skills, the books in the Lindie Lou Adventure Series transform from a colorful read-aloud to an independent read. Readers who excel at a young age will enjoy the age-appropriate story line.

Librarians can introduce the Lindie Lou Adventure Series to their students and teachers. The book series follows guidelines recommended by the **Common Core Standards for English Language Arts.**

Students like to read the book in many formats. Audio and e-book versions are available on the website. Young students also enjoy seeing the book projected on a large screen. They can follow the words and watch the color illustrations. This helps bring the story to life. Many students like to pick their favorite characters.

The Lindie Lou Adventure Series is also a perfect read for English-as-a-second-language students. The vocabulary and descriptions are well written and easy to understand.

Collaboration among parents, teachers, and librarians guides young readers to the joy of reading. The amazing world of adventure is often first introduced to children through books.

The Lindie Lou Adventure Series is a literary tool. The books are ideal for parents and teachers to read aloud, engaging for independent readers, and are colorful early chapter books for library users.

Adventure Series

- ## Book 1: FLYING HIGH
  Flying on an Airplane for the Very First Time!

Lindie Lou is a curious puppy who dreams of seeing the world. She lives in a "Puppy Playground" with her brothers and sisters. One day, Lindie Lou learns she is being adopted by a family who lives far-away. Soon she is "Flying High" on an airplane for the very first time!

- ## Book 2: UP IN SPACE
  An Adventure at the Space Needle!

Follow Lindie Lou through the city of Seattle, where she meets-up with an old friend, meets new friends and learns life lessons along the way. Join in the fun when Lindie Lou discovers Rachel the Pig, sees flying fish, orca whales and the gum wall. But her biggest adventure awaits... when she goes UP IN SPACE.

- ## Book 3: HARVEST TIME
  Celebration on an Organic Farm!

Lindie Lou has no idea what an organic farm is like. While visiting Cousin Ronda, she discovers a whole new way of living. Join in the fun! Lindie Lou enjoys the thrill of a hayloft, the challenge of a corn maze, the celebration of the harvest, and the dangers of a combine. Her family and friends play together, solve problems together, even save each other's lives!

- ## Book 4 : BIG CITY MAGIC
  Uncover the Secret of the Big Apple!

Guess where Lindie Lou finds the big apple?
Hint...it's in a city called "The Big Apple."
Send us your guesses to... www.lindielou.com/blog.html

About the Author and the Illustrator

JEANNE BENDER
Author

Jeanne Bender loves to travel. While exploring the world, she experienced many incredible things. Bender decided to write about her adventures through the eyes of her puppy Lindie Lou.

Lindie Lou traveled with author Jeanne Bender to many places around the world. Their experiences became the inspiration of the *Lindie Lou Adventure Series*.

Bender's education began early on when she received high praise for her poetry and early composition. Later she studied with a creative writing professor in Seattle, Washington, and continued her education in the United Kingdom at Oxford University.

Bender's beginning chapter books titled the *Lindie Lou Adventure Series,* were first introduced to elementary school students grades K-5.

Bender first experienced *"**Lindie Lou mania"*** when students told her they loved her stories and the characters wanted to read more about them. Everywhere Bender went she was humbled when children lined up to buy her books.

KATE WILLOWS
Illustrator

Kate Willows loves drawing and coloring things on her computer. She creates animals and cartoons for everyone to enjoy, including all the Lindie Lou characters.

Willows graduated from The Ohio State University with a degree in art technology and a minor in design. Kate also works for a gaming company and does amazing drawings.

She enjoys playing video games and reading in her spare time. Kate lives near Columbus, Ohio, with her two cats Nyx and Nico.